THE CAPTAIN'S CAT

STEFON MEARS

Thousand
Faces
Publishing

Also by Stefon Mears

The Rise of Magic Series
Magician's Choice
Sleight of Mind
Lunar Alchemy
Three Fae Monte
The Sphinx Principle
Double Backed Magic
Mercury Fold (forthcoming)

Cavan Oltblood Series
Half a Wizard
The Ice Dagger
Spells of Undeath

Power City Tales
Not Quite Bulletproof
No Money in Heroism

Standalones
The Hireling
The Captain's Cat
Save Whiskers!
The Ogre of Threepeaks
Between the Cracks
Sects and the City
Prince of a Thousand Worlds
Devil's Night
Portal-Land, Oregon
Stealing from Pirates
Fade to Gold
With a Broken Sword
Twice Against the Dragon
The House on Cedar Street
Sudden Death
On the Edge of Faerie

Short Story Collections
Spell Slingers
Twisted Timelines
Longhairs and Short Tales: A Collection of Cat Stories
Dangerous Space
Confronting Legends (Spells & Swords Vol. 1)
The Patreon Collection, Vol. 1-8 (Vol. 9, coming soon)

Nonfiction
The 30-Day Novel and Beyond!

Spells for Hire Series
Devil's Shoestring
Zombie Powder
Spirit Trap
Dragon's Blood

The Telepath Trilogy
Surviving Telepathy
Immoral Telepathy
Targeting Telepathy

Edge of Humanity Series
Caught Between Monsters
Hunting Monsters

Jumpstart Duchy Series
Into the Torn Kingdoms
The Dragon's Gold
The Gift Castle
The Deadly Feast
The King's Test
Triumph in the Torn Kingdoms

Published by Thousand Faces Publishing, Portland, Oregon

http://1kfaces.com

ISBN: 978-1-948490-50-4

THE CAPTAIN'S CAT

1

―――――――

The worst sound in the world jerked Carbine awake.

Oh, it was *loud*.

Louder than those giant box-movers. Louder than any of the two-legs yelling at each other. Even louder than Scruffy, the heavy two-legs who'd sneak Carbine treats when no one else was looking.

Scruffy could get very angry at the other two-legs. And when she yowled, the sound came close to hurting Carbine's sensitive ears.

But this.

This.

This shrieking-buzzing-honking thing.

Yanked Carbine *right* out of one of his favorite sunbeam dreams. And it had the *audacity* to *keep going*.

Shrieking-buzzing-honking. At volumes that made even Scruffy's worst tantrum sound like a gentle, happy purr.

And it was flashing an angry light, too.

Well, this would never do. Not at all.

Carbine would teach that stupid shrieking-buzzing-honking thing a lesson.

Hard to pinpoint where it was coming from. Too loud. Too sharp. Might be everywhere at once.

No. No it was coming from somewhere up the walls...

There!

That light. Oh, that flashing light. It was high up on the wall. And *it* was making that horrible sound.

Home probably would've thought it was too high for Carbine to reach. But Home didn't know how high Carbine could jump. When he felt like it.

And that shrieking-buzzing-honking thing, that was what Carbine called *serious motivation.*

So Carbine rolled to his paws. His sleek, fluffy white fur all rumpled and out of sorts from what *had been* an excellent nap.

No time even to bathe. Not with that evil racket blaring.

No. Lesson time for the noisy flashing light.

Carbine jumped down from the big, comfy bed he shared with Home.

He trotted across the smooth floor. Too smooth. Full-out running was a bad idea in most of Carbine's domain. Too easy to do something *no one should ever see.*

Cats did not slip. And anyone who said otherwise was a dirty liar. And needed a lesson in manners at least as big as the one Carbine had planned for that blaring flashing thing.

The blaring flashing thing, though, it was high up the wall.

Very high.

Higher than even Carbine could jump. Which was pretty darned high, if he said so himself.

Carbine winced at the foul racket as he considered his options.

There was the shelf that Home sat at, with his boxes. The skinny little things he wasted so much potential petting time on.

That shelf was a good height. And unless Carbine was mistaken he smelled...

He withheld judgment until he leapt up. A leap so quick and elegant that he was almost sorry there were no witnesses.

But yes. Home had left in a hurry, leaving some juice behind from his last meal. Meat juice, from some strange animal that wasn't chicken, but smelled and tasted a lot like chicken anyway.

Carbine almost left the juice where it was. Home didn't eat enough. Home might need that juice later...

No. Carbine needed it now. For the jump.

Because putting an end to that flashing blaring light, and that shrieking-buzzing-honking sound, well, that had *paramount importance.*

So Carbine spared a few precious seconds to fortify himself with tasty not-quite-chicken juice.

Too well cooked, and flavored with some kind of boring plant life that didn't deserve to grace the flesh of a prey animal.

But a good taste nonetheless.

Carbine turned and surveyed this portion of his domain.

The offender sat high up on the wall. Past the part of the wall that opened whenever Carbine needed it to.

But the offender crouched close to the six fun shelves.

Home didn't like it when Carbine played on the fun shelves. Knocking over this and that.

Honestly, though, if Home *really meant* for Carbine not to jump onto those shelves, then he shouldn't have put so many portable and shiny things on them.

No time for play on the fun shelves.

Carbine had a mission. A mission even more important than bathing.

A Top. Priority. Mission.

Carbine moved to the edge of the meal shelf.

Gauged the distance to the fun shelves.

Hadn't changed since last time. Good.

Still. A fairly long jump. Not too long for Carbine, of course. And yet. Long enough to merit proper attention.

Carbine knew well the value of caution. Especially when distracted by evil flashing lights and even fouler horrible sounds.

So he bobbed in place. Checking the distance. Checking the arc. Checking the feel of his muscles.

Yes. His body remembered right. There would be no problems.

Carbine lowered himself. Prepped.

Jumped!

A perfect landing. Of course. Right on the third fun shelf up from the floor. Exactly as he'd intended.

Well.

All right.

Since no one else was around, he could admit that the racket and flashing had thrown him off. A little. No more than that.

So yes, maybe his hip bumped that series of smelly old boxes that opened on three sides, revealing a series of many thin crinklies that Home could stare at for hours.

But they just were stupid boxes anyway. So who cared if they ended up at a funny angle? And if maybe one of them fell to the floor with a thump.

After all, the thump was pretty much lost under all the racket anyway. Right?

The point was, Carbine was on the third shelf up.

And from there, easy as wall-opening to go shelf-to-shelf up all the way to the top. Forepaws onto the new shelf, then a hop. Then pick the next spot and go.

Nothing else even knocked over. Which meant, really, that Home would have no right to complain.

If anything, Home should be pleased to share his life with such a nimble, agile wonder as Carbine.

Up here on the top shelf were only three shiny things. The ones Home most valued (after Carbine, of course). Weird shaped things that stood upright. All of them clear enough to see through, but made the world look funny if Carbine bothered.

He rarely did. They didn't smell or taste interesting enough.

Carbine lost a moment sniffing at them all the same. He longed to knock one to the floor.

But the shrieking-buzzing-honking thing would simply *not let up*.

And it was even louder, this close up. Each shrieking-buzzing-honk hurt Carbine's ears.

It had to be dealt with. Immediately.

Carbine walked to the edge of the shelf.

Yes. A very short jump to it now.

It was small. Perhaps half Carbine's size. Rounded. Looked smooth, too.

Yes. It was big enough. Carbine could do it.

He bobbed three times to gauge the distance. Even for a short jump, caution was called for when he faced a rounded, smooth landing zone.

Carbine jumped.

Almost went over. But caught himself.

Carbine now stood *on* the flashy noisy evil thing. Winced against its incessant cries.

He proceeded to smack it hard, claws out.

Two. Three. Four times!

It failed to accept that it was beaten. Continued to flash and shriek-buzz-honk.

This called for major action.

Carbine tried to bite it.

It was too wide. Too smooth. No place to sink in his deadly fangs.

It kept up those awful, painful sounds.

Well, claws would have to do the job.

He smacked it several times in quick succession. The same series of blows that had defeated the Tabby of Beta Seven.

Silence?

Yes!

Sweet silence.

A moment of happy bliss for Carbine, and a tale for the ages. How he'd overcome...

Wait...

That thing was *still flashing*.

Well, then it still had a lesson to learn, didn't it?

Carbine smacked it several more times.

The thing failed to admit defeat. It *would not relent*.

Fine then.

Home would *have* to stop whatever he was doing and solve this urgent problem.

Yes, Carbine had silenced the awful beast. But certainly he could not be expected to tolerate that flashing light when he was trying to enjoy a good nap.

Carbine jumped back over to the shelves, and made his way quickly down to the floor.

He turned and trotted for the section of wall that opened whenever he needed it to.

Yes. He would find Home. And Home would make it better.

2

———

A breach alert was nothing to mess with.

Bolan and his team trotted double-time through the wide passages of the *Quick Sail*.

Their idiot of a quartermaster should've taken the word of an experienced security sergeant and given Bolan's team berths amidships. Quickest possible route to any problems.

Instead, he'd stuck them back by the cargo holds, with Conray's team. Two decks down and too damn far away.

Might've been convenient if the pirates had hit the ship near the cargo bays. But they hadn't. Word was, the breach pod landed sunside. Damn close to the bridge.

Those bastards didn't just want cargo. Not if they were hitting close to the bridge. Which meant they weren't pirates at all.

They were worse.

Ship thieves.

Captain Harnan better have a trick or two up his famous sleeve...

And he'd be more than welcome to silence that goddamn breach alert any time now. All action alerts were bad, but breach alerts were the loudest. The most piercing.

Anyone sleeping through this racket had to be—

"God! That thing's loud enough to wake the dead!" Mackenzie bitched. Sounded ready to shoot the nearest alert beacon.

Bolan understood the urge. But she looked like it hurt her ears even more than his. Probably her own fault. Mackenzie liked her potables a little stronger than most. And since she wasn't supposed to be on shift right now, she'd probably hit the bottle harder than she'd needed to over third watch. In the name of a good time.

Still. She'd armored up fast enough, when the breach alert sounded.

Though fast, in this case, was too slow. Someone was cutting through the hull right now.

Couldn't be helped. New armor. Dark green flexiplate. Heavier than their old gear, but as good against slugthrowers and chemshot as it was against hard rad and lasers.

Well worth the weight.

Their hard beam rifles were the same ones they'd had for the last four missions. Same ones Bolan'd been drilling them on for a good year now.

New armor might slow them down, but they'd shoot straight at least.

So hungover or not Mackenzie had readied at speed, and now she kept formation. Third pair back of six. Kept in step with the others. And moved quick enough down the passage.

And a little crack like hers wasn't cause enough for Bolan to censure her.

So he settled for a "Quiet on ranks!" and pushed his squad a little faster.

Their first rotation on this merchant ship. Passages a little wider than most. Bad and good. Good for moving security through the ship at speed from all the way back by the freaking cargo holds.

Bad, because boarders got the same benny.

Doors were flat to the walls. No cover, when the shooting started.

Metal decks. No quiet ceramic coating. Rang out with their heavy combat boots. The breachers would hear them coming a klick away. Couldn't be helped.

Might even be an edge. The squad probably sounded like a whole battalion.

The passages might've been wide, but gunmetal gray was a bad color choice for the bulkheads. Too dark, even under the runner lights, and the flashing alert.

Too easy to hide things on gunmetal gray.

Slap grenades, for example. Bolan'd seen slap grenades used all too effectively, back in the Commons War, on surfaces dark as these.

Hard place to fight, this ship. But at least his squad had full bellies, bunks, and a good payday coming when they reached Carnan Eleven.

And a fight meant Bolan would get to blood his squad's three rookies.

Bolan and his team cut single-file across a tight engineering passage. By the time they ascended another deck and turned bridgeward, someone cut the sound on the flashing red action alert.

"Thank god!" Mackenzie said. Too loud.

"Last warning, Mac," Bolan barked. "I said quiet."

Bolan had walked every passage on the ship, back at dock. Got the layout in his muscles, not just his head. They were two turns, but only maybe another fifty meters from—

"What the—"

First rank spaceside tripped and went down. Darius. Vet of three runs and two firefights, but no wars.

His soldiers threw their backs against bulkheads. Divided the ranks.

Rifles came down. Ready. Some aimed low.

Then Bolan spotted it.

White, fluffy and running his way.

Bolan gave the high, sharp, warning whistle.

Rifle barrels jerked up at speed.

"Just the captain's cat," he barked at them.

"God, I almost shot it."

That last came from Orin. One of the rookies. Still had rockfeet –

weak in low and zero gee – and still unbloodied, but a crack shot at the range.

"You harm that cat, expect to suck vacuum," Mackenzie said. Looking as though she would've spaced him herself for the crime.

"What?" Orin actually sounded shocked.

"That's the captain's cat and we're at high space," Bolan said. "You shoot that beast and the captain's likely to space whatever's left after I'm done with you."

Orin's eyes widened. Boy needed to check his regs. Killing a ship's cat at high space was no joke.

"How'd it get out of his cabin?"

Boy, this kid *was* a rockfoot. Was this his first rotation off a planet?

Bolan didn't need to answer. Mackenzie did it for him.

"Because he's the *captain's cat*. He has a door tag on his collar, and he gets the run of the ship."

"But the alert—"

"Darius," Bolan called. "Nap time's over. On your feet. Move it, soldiers! We got a fight coming."

Darius moved too slow in the new armor. They all did. Bolan would have to institute full-armor drills, once this action was over.

But first, he needed to get his team in place to stop that breach.

3

─────────

Carbine had barely gotten out through the wall when a two-legs almost kicked him.

Him! Carbine!

Now that was the sort of behavior Carbine had no patience with. And if someone *important* had dared to do such a thing – and if it had been someone *important* then it would have been an accident, which would've been understandable, for the two-legs were not nearly as graceful as even the least cat, let alone so fine an example of feline splendor as Carbine – well, then Carbine would've had no choice but to smack or nip.

Something quick. Not too painful. But a lesson. A clear, concise lesson. So they would learn. So they would remember that Carbine was not a cat to be taken lightly. That he was swift and strong and beautiful and fearsome. That he was to be *cherished*.

And not ever to be *kicked*.

Not. Ever.

But this two-legs wasn't anyone. Just one of the carapace two-legs. Hard bodies. No faces. Just a smooth, curved sheet of carapace where the face would be on a proper two-legs.

In fact, a whole pack of carapace two-legs were here for some reason.

Carbine didn't care much for the carapace two-legs.

They didn't smell quite right. Oh, they smelled like they'd been eating the right food. *Pride* food. The food eaten by each of the two-legs that Home insisted on bringing into Carbine's domain for extended periods of time.

But these carapace two-legs, they also smelled of fear and excitement and sleep. Of fornication in a couple of cases, and one of them smelled strongly like ... like the liquid in one of the clear shinies on the fun shelves, second shelf from the top, third shiny from the right...

Point was, none of these carapace two-legs were *important*.

And the two-legs who'd *almost* kicked Carbine, well, at least he'd had the good sense to pull his foot aside at the last moment. To trip himself, rather than dare strike at the magnificent glory that was Carbine's person. Rather than dare to face Carbine's wrath.

So that much was proper, at least.

And the two-legs had fallen to the floor. Perhaps in obeisance. Which would also be proper.

But Carbine had no time for carapace two-legs. Not even one offering obeisance for the wrong he had nearly done Carbine.

No. Carbine had a mission. He had to find Home and solve the problem of the flashing noise monster that interrupted his nap.

And the problem was even worse than Carbine had known. The flashing noise monster had not just its own pride, but what were clearly *littermates* out here.

Many of them. Carbine could see them. Always perching high along the walls. Out of easy pouncing range.

But the lesson Carbine had taught their leader must've spread through its littermates. Because though they still insisted on flashing their bright lights as though they were themselves important – possibly even considering themselves of equal importance with Carbine, which was obviously ridiculous – they at least had the good sense to hold back their shrieking-buzzing-honking clamor.

Still. Carbine had to put a stop to them. His entire domain was under threat.

Home would know what to do.

The most recent smell of Home, Carbine thought, tracked back the direction the carapace two-legs had come from. So Carbine took advantage of the parted forest of their legs and began trotting that direction while the carapace two-legs meowed and yowled at each other.

Likely they were censuring that one carapace two-legs for his near-kicking of Carbine. That would be good and proper. They should be firm with him. But not too severe. He had, after all, tripped himself instead of *actually* kicking Carbine.

And certainly, a near-kicking should not be punished as harshly as an *actual* kicking.

Carbine would leave the offending two-legs to the justice of what appeared to be its littermates.

He headed off down the passage, following what might be the strongest scent of Home.

Carbine reached one of the many-directions spots. Here, he could keep moving the same direction. He could turn to his right or his left. He could descend deeper or ascend higher, along ramps.

But which direction led to Home?

That was the real question, and it had no easy answer. An uncertainty that, unfortunately, was Carbine's own fault.

He'd been, perhaps, too generous. He'd allowed Home free run of the entire domain. Spoiled him that way, really.

No. No. Home was worth it. There was no better two-legs to be found anywhere. Home deserved the freedom to wander and hunt as he chose.

Unfortunately, right now, that freedom meant Home's smell led in every direction.

So. Where scent-tracking might not avail him, Carbine would turn his powerful mind to deduction.

Home, of course, had chosen a scattering of his own favorite places, away from their den. Which was right and proper, really, and demonstrated that Home was a discerning two-legs. Fully capable of finding spots of maximum comfort and happiness, supplementary to the joys of their den.

But those favorite places were scattered across Carbine's domain.

Which of them would Home choose right now?

Oh, at other times of day, that question would be easily solved. Home followed patterns in his movements, after all. Same as any two-legs.

But this was Carbine's daily nap time. And embarrassing as this was to admit – even to himself – Carbine had gotten lax. He'd grown so used to his own routines and his comfortable domain that he'd stopped worrying about where Home went during something as simple as nap time.

Then again, this wasn't a simple nap time. The flashing noise monsters were attacking, weren't they?

True, they didn't seem to pose much of a physical threat. Not to Carbine, at least. But then, doubtless it was obvious even to them that they could offer no true threat to Carbine's glory. Save for shrieking-buzzing-honking at him.

But what if their noise and clamor had frightened Home?

What if he wasn't in one of his favorite spots? What if he'd run away and hidden?

Would Home do that? Could he be hiding someplace? Frightened? Waiting for his Carbine to come rescue him?

No.

No, Home was strong, and Home was brave. Surely he would not be hiding, panicked by something as small as the flashing noise monster.

And even if he were, the ringing of their silence surely proved that they could be beaten.

No. Home was not cowering somewhere. There could be no doubt that Home was acting even now in defense of their domain.

Such a good two-legs.

Where would he be defending? Where could the flashing noise monsters pose the most threat?

Their food!

Of course. It was so obvious, now that Carbine was free of that awful racket and that forest of carapace two-legs.

The flashing noise monsters might threaten their food. Ergo, Home would be *defending* their food, right at the source.

Yes. That made sense.

With a destination in mind now, Carbine began trotting purposefully through his marvelously broad (but far too smooth) halls.

4

Overhead lights were off in the galley, but Engurasoff was considering turning them on. True, he could see his station well enough by the small, red cook lights – plus the rhythmic flashing of the alert light – but he'd see the whole of the galley better if he turned the lights on. Could keep better track of whether or not Song was getting her work done fast enough right now.

Of course, turning on the galley lights while the ship had boarders was against regs. But how much would that matter anyway, once they started cooking? The savory smells would tell anyone nearby that they were in here.

Which would even be good, if it were the crew smelling them at work. Admittedly, though, if it were those pirates...

Well, then, maybe Engurasoff would have someone to vent his frustrations on.

There was just no way to make proper sourdough in space. No matter how he fiddled with the environmental controls or how high quality the starter dough he bought, it just never came out right.

It wouldn't thicken right, in mixing. And it simply *would not* rise properly, no matter what he did to it.

And damn it, right now the sandwiches he had in mind really needed proper sourdough.

What he had in his hands was as close as he could get. Still wasn't thick enough. And it didn't sound right when he slapped it down on the cutting board.

So Engurasoff pounded it and beat it with his big, meaty fists, and he slapped it against his cutting board again and again. Sprinkling flour as needed. Every movement trying to *force* that dough closer to proper sourdough consistency than it really wanted to get, given the improper climate aboard the *Quick Sail*.

Aboard any ship, really.

Artificial gravity and environmentals were great for humans. But they just were not real enough to persuade certain doughs and mixes to behave the way they did on planets.

To Engurasoff's endless frustration.

"Chief," Song said for the fourth time. Engurasoff could've said the rest of her words with her. "We're *supposed* to be bunkered down with the rest of the crew."

"Security's not bunkered down," Engurasoff said letting some of his dough frustration creep into his voice. Or maybe just some of his frustration with Song. She was a good assistant ship's cook. The best of his four assistants, really.

But she had her priorities all *wrong* for this job. And she had to learn.

"Bridge crew's not bunkered down, either," he continued, while pounding his dough. "Neither's engineering. Or—"

"They all have *duties* during an action alert," she insisted. And worse, she was turning away from her turkey to point from him to herself and back again. "We don't. We're *supposed* to bunker down. Our *orders* are to *bunker down.*"

He gave her a dark glare and forcefully pointed at her station.

Skinny little thing that she was – too skinny for a ship's cook, really. Who'd ever trust her food, skinny as she was? – she rolled her eyes and huffed with her shoulders, but she turned back to the turkey she was prepping for a quickbake for his sandwiches.

The three other stations were empty. The other primary assistant ship's cooks were bunkered down by Engurasoff's order. The way Song seemed to believe *they* should've been bunkered down.

But she had much to learn if she ever wanted to be any ship's chief cook.

"Oh, we have our action duties too, Song," Engurasoff said. "Don't you believe we don't. Even if ours aren't enumerated in the regs."

"But—"

"You're young," he said. "You've never faced an *action* alert before, let alone a *breach* alert. I have. And let me tell you. *Nothing* burns food like fighting. And we don't know how long the fight's going to last. What we do here — these sandwiches we make — may save crew lives. May even swing the battle."

He frowned at her. "And you're not using enough oregano. Again. And the pepper—"

"What's wrong with my pepper?"

"It's the wrong blend for turkey. You want the finer grain for turkey and chicken. Coarser grain for—"

"This isn't real turkey anyway."

"WELL WE BETTER MAKE THEM BELIEVE IT IS!" he roared at her. "They're out there risking their lives to save ours. And when they bite into what we give them, I want that first bite to make them feel glad to be alive. I want them thinking we snuck a *real* turkey in here and killed it just for this fight. I want them—"

"All right, all right," she said, turning back to her turkey. "I'll wash it again and—"

"Don't you waste my spices. Just correct for the future. And add some more oregano, damn it."

"Yes, Chief," she said, but sounded a little more respectful about it, at least.

"And when you finish with the turkey, start in on the tomatoes."

"You don't mean—"

"Yes, I mean the real tomatoes."

"That's why the fake turkey's—"

"You call it *turkey* on my ship. Even if it never hatched from an egg."

"But that's why it's so important, right? You're going to give them real tomatoes and lettuce."

"Damn right I am," Engurasoff said firmly. "And you save every one of those tomato seeds. I'm going to get vegetables to grow on this ship if it's the last thing I do."

Song frowned at what he was working in his hands. "That's never going to pass for sourdough."

Engurasoff slapped down his dough and turned toward her, murder in his eyes.

"Mrrr-oww?"

Oh, no. Why did the captain have to give his cat access to *all* doors? Cats had no place in a *galley*.

But sure enough, there was the little white fuzz bucket. Standing tall and proud. Tail high, as though they hadn't been chased by pirates for the last hour. As though there wasn't a breach pod somewhere on their hull.

"Awww," Song said, crouching down and wiggling her fingers to draw the cat's attention. "You looking for snacks or love, little guy?"

Of course the cat trotted right over to her. Immediately started licking at the raw turkeyish taste on her hands and fingers.

Song, alas, was young enough to be charmed by this.

"You know what else that cat licks, right?" Engurasoff said.

Song gave him a sour look. "Don't be gross."

"Right," Engurasoff turned from his dough and scooped up the cat.

"Hey, wait," Song said, looking troubled. "We can't let him go back out there. What if something happens to him?"

Engurasoff stopped, halfway to the door. Cat squirming in his hands.

"You're right," he said with a sigh. "We better— Hey!"

The cat shoved off Engurasoff's chest with strong back paws. He hit the floor smoothly and raced for the door.

"Catch him!" Song said, sounding more worried about the cat than her turkey, which *proved* that her priorities were skewed.

The door slid open for the cat, of course, and he was already halfway through the mess hall by the time Engurasoff reached the doorway.

He shook his head. "We'll never catch the fool thing. And even if we did, how could we hold it?"

"We could take him and bunker down."

"Leave off that," Engurasoff said sharply. "We have a job to do."

"But what about the cat?" Song said. "Maybe we could catch him and remove his door tag."

Engurasoff scoffed. "Any other ship maybe. But you do that to Captain *Harnan's* cat and you'll be *lucky* if all you lose is your job."

"But we'd be trying to—"

"Doesn't matter," Engurasoff said, shaking his head. "Cat's some kind of good luck piece for the captain. And restricting the cat's movements is like restricting his own luck."

"So the poor thing's on his own?"

"Fine," Engurasoff said with a heavy sigh. "Main comms are down, but computers are still up. I can type something up to send to the bridge. Let them know we just saw the captain's cat, and he left, heading burnward. Not much else we can do."

"But—"

"But *nothing*." Engurasoff pointed at her station. "We have hungry men and women to feed. Now *wash your hands* and get back to work."

5

———————

IN ENTIRELY TOO MUCH OF A HURRY, CARBINE LEFT THE FOOD PLACE AND started back out into the wider expanse of his domain. Up high on the dark walls, the flashing noise monsters mocked him with their flashing.

Well, Surly was certainly in high dudgeon today. And Carbine did not like that.

No, he did not like that one bit.

Being picked up would've been fine. If it had been followed by some *proper* attention. Petting. Cooing. Treats, maybe.

Treats would've been lovely. Perhaps some of that strange, yet tasty bird Carbine had tasted on Svelte's fingers.

Carbine liked Svelte. She was *always* nice to him. Friendly tones, scritching, the occasional treat.

Surly, on the other hand, always treated Carbine as though Carbine had done something terrible. Or perhaps was *about* to do something terrible.

As though that could possibly happen.

Well. While Surly's behavior that day would have been improper in *anyone*, let alone a two-legs in *Carbine's* domain, he supposed that in some cases, allowances had to be made.

After all, it was quite clear from the smells that Surly was responsible for feeding Home. Which Carbine was definitely in favor of.

Furthermore, Surly *might* even have been responsible for Carbine's food too. Though he was less certain of that.

And even if not, perhaps Surly's fits of pique could be tolerated. For Home's sake.

But forcibly wrangling Carbine's person like that? Oh, no, no, no. That would never do at all.

Honestly, Surly should consider himself lucky that Carbine did nothing more than leap down.

He *had*, after all, briefly considered teaching Surly a quick lesson in manners. Nothing permanent of course, let alone fatal. No, not to the one providing food for Home. But a lesson all the same.

Carbine had though, in the end, decided against it. Giving Surly a lesson just then would've upset Svelte. And it might've upset Home.

What was more, Surly, considering his mood, might not have understood the lesson.

Surly could be a bit slow to learn, even for a two-legs.

And anyway, clearly Home was not there. Which meant that the flashing noise monsters – despite their silent, flashing presence – were not a threat to the food.

Good.

Nothing must ever threaten the food. Just as nothing must ever threaten the den.

Some things were just sacrosanct, and even considering the possibility of them being under threat agitated Carbine enough that he really did need to stop and soothe himself with a proper bath.

But he didn't have time for that. The threat of the flashing noise monsters *had* to be dealt with. And that they were not *yet* threatening the food didn't mean it wasn't part of their agenda.

They did, after all, have littermates watching over Surly and Svelte as they...

Those two weren't preparing food *for* the flashing noise monsters, were they?

No. No, Surly might've been in high dudgeon, but Svelte was

relaxed. Irritated about something, perhaps, but she'd cheered up at once on seeing Carbine.

Carbine had smelled hardly any fear from them. Not even as much as he'd smelled from the carapace two-legs. So they couldn't have felt threatened by the presence of the flashing noise monsters.

Perhaps their morale had rallied after Carbine's great defeat of the monsters' king in single combat. Forcing both it *and* its littermates to lose their voices and dwell in silence.

Yes. That must've been it. They must've known that Carbine had already won a great victory for their pride. Gained much-needed confidence from his swift, decisive action.

Of course! And now they were preparing food for the pride as though nothing were wrong. As though the flashing noise monsters presented no threat at all!

Oh, brave Surly and Svelte! Carbine might sing a song in their honor later.

Perhaps even...

Yes. Carbine would magnanimously forgive Surly his high dudgeon.

Even though they were still polluting perfectly good prey fowl with plants.

Surely they had to know that plants were only good for two things.

Parts of some plants were solid enough to give a good crunch. Felt marvelous on the teeth.

Others could help Carbine throw up. If he needed to.

Really, other than offering interesting smells, that was all that plants had to offer the world. Especially here in Carbine's domain, where there was never any hot sun he might desire shade from.

Of course, hot sun also provided wonderful sunbeams, and—

Enough distractions.

Carbine still needed to find Home.

If Home felt his place wasn't defending the food, where would he go?

Unfortunately, Home's ways weren't always clear to Carbine. No matter how much time he devoted to studying his favorite two-legs.

No. No excuses for Carbine. He was a clever cat. Cleverer than any two-legs, surely.

Yes. He could figure out where Home had gone.

If Home weren't defending the food – and he wasn't – then…

Was he attacking?

Surely not. Surely Home was smart enough to come get Carbine if he needed to fight something. They were much better together, after all, and Home was smart enough to know that.

No, Home could not be fighting the flashing noise monsters yet.

So that meant he was…

Consulting with other two-legs?

He certainly did do that frequently. Some of it, of course, was just for the companionship of his own kind. Carbine could understand that. He sometimes wished for another cat to share his pride and domain with.

A mate, perhaps. Or one who could be his brother from another litter.

But Home had his pick of possible mates and chosen brothers from the whole of the pride.

Who were Home's favorite two-legs?

Scruffy?

Scruffy!

Of course! That list had to start with Scruffy. And maybe it didn't need to go any further.

Scruffy wasn't just good to Carbine. Scruffy's company often brought Home pleasure and happiness. They'd never mated, for some reason, but they often spent ages mewling at each other until they made that happy sound that only two-legs made. The one that sounded like a staggered yowl, but a happy yowl.

Of course, a happy yowl was kind of an odd idea, just on its own. But the two-legs always seemed to need to express everything verbally.

They had meows and mewls and yowls and hisses for all occasions. Probably because they weren't as good at body language.

Not their fault, though. They could be sweet creatures, but they lacked many of the gifts that Bast had given to cats alone.

The point was, Home might well have gone to consult with Scruffy about the flashing noise monsters. And Scruffy was always easy to find.

She only had two favorite places in Carbine's domain, and spent the vast majority of her time in only one of them.

The Humming Place.

The Humming Place was interesting. Its walls had many shelves and projections Carbine could jump onto.

Though, admittedly, Scruffy seemed to worry whenever Carbine did that. As though he might fall and hurt himself. Silly, really.

And the Humming Place was full of clicks and whirs and hums of many volumes and tones. And spots that vibrated sometimes, too.

And ... and it was full of *flashing lights*!

Of course!

Little ones here and there. Some of them solid, but often a *noise* would change and a *light* would *flash*!

How had Carbine not thought of this in the first place?

The nap. Yes. The nap was to blame. It, and the sunbeam dream, were simply too pleasant. Perhaps Carbine was only now truly waking up...

Be that as it may, the answer was obvious. Scruffy knew *lots* about flashing lights and strange noises. She had to know all there was to know about the flashing noise monsters.

Naturally, Home would go consult with her. And he would do so in the Humming Place.

Carbine trotted off the right direction. It was a fair distance from the food place, but he knew the way. And that was what really mattered.

6

Conray hated the new armor. Too heavy. In a battle, speed was often more important than a little extra protection. And that added weight on the arms of her shooters, that might throw off their aim at a critical moment.

The lieutenant had to know that. Surely he did. He was an old ground pounder himself. Which meant that Blabbermouth Bolan must've gotten in his ear.

Damn that Bolan anyway. Just because *he* was getting old didn't mean the rest of them were.

Hell, the extra protection was probably just an excuse. Bolan's old armor probably didn't fit right anymore. Not since he'd started taking seconds on dessert. Probably wanted the new armor so he didn't have go all shamefaced and ask to have his old armor refit.

Pride. More battles were lost to pride than ignorance. And that was a damned shame.

The color sucked too. Dark green was a bad color for flexiplate in the first place. And any kind of green stood out against these gunmetal gray bulkheads and decks.

Made them entirely too easy a group of targets under the flashing alert light. On a ship that offered precious little cover.

No helping that. This was a merchant vessel. Designed, apparently, without any thought spared for repelling boarders.

Which raised another question. Just what the hell was *famous* Captain Harnan hauling, anyway? Even this close to the cargo bays, there was an odd smell to the air. Metallic, and maybe a touch ... greasy?

Whatever it was, it had to be a big deal to *somebody*.

Because it turned out the boarders came in two breach pods.

Two!

Conray and her team had been halfway to the bridge when word came that they had to turn around and get back to the cargo bays. Where they'd started.

Lots of pointless running about in too-heavy armor.

Two breach pods...

The L.T. said there'd only been the one pirate ship pinging the sensors. So just how big was that ship, that they carried enough spare crew to fill *two* breach pods with boarding parties?

No. Wasn't just crew size. Had to be something more going on here. Otherwise they would've timed one of the breach pods for distraction, or landed both in a decent crossfire position.

But they hadn't. One was back here at the emergency hatch near cargo bay one. The other was all the way up near the bridge.

That meant the division was about objectives.

That meant they had to be after the ship itself, *plus* the cargo.

Well, not on *Conray's* watch.

Because of the lack of cover, she'd pulled her squad back up the narrow escape passage. Set them up here at the nearest intersection. Six points of cover here. The wide main passages, plus a pair of engineering tunnels, and ramps updecks or downdecks.

Added bonus, this position gave her and her dozen shooters six different fire lines down that emergency passage.

She had to laugh about that.

Conray had righteously bitched about all the intersections when she'd first come aboard the *Quick Sail*.

How many cross-passages did one ship need anyway? Just how

lazy were these civilian engineers that they couldn't be arsed to get things done in tubes, like they did in the navy?

But now, she found herself grateful for all those intersections. Not as good as proper shields and breach cover, but plenty of ways to handle a fighting retreat, if needed.

Though even that was a mixed blessing. If her squad had to fall back, the boarders could break free other directions into the rest of the ship...

Damn the probabilities anyway. Only six months out of the corps, and Conray had never felt more homesick than she did the moment that breach alert sounded.

This was the wrong kind of ship for this engagement. And she had the wrong kind of squad.

Oh, her people were ... competent enough at the range and in port. But they were no marines. Didn't have enough experience. Didn't have enough nerve. Thought more about their next shore leave than about survival and objectives *right now*.

Well, Conray would whip them into shape. And maybe a little action would help. Maybe getting shot at – first time for some of them – would jar their little worlds enough to make them harder. Tougher.

And if not, well, they better sell their lives dear.

She could hear the hiss of boarding party's cutter now. Working on the emergency hatch.

Hah! Score one for Conray's side. They hadn't been able to hack in. Maybe *some* of the things people said about that Captain Harnan were true after all...

Conray sniffed the air. Smelled like ... sour ozone. Poly cutters, then. Worked off a combination of lasers, diamonds, and tight, tight beam hard rad.

Tricky to work with. Take some time too.

Oh, what Conray would give for a pair of slap grenades right now. Even two of them, placed right on these dark, gunmetal bulkheads and decks, would be enough to take out half a boarding party. Easy.

But no. Conray wasn't much more than a *civilian* now. And *civil-*

ians weren't even supposed to *know* about slap grenades. Much less *use* them.

Too bad.

She heard the click on her helmet speaker. Warning of an incoming transmission.

L.T.'s deep voice. Sounded agitated. "Attention all sec teams. Two breach pods confirmed." *Duh.* "Squads Red and Blue in place?"

"Red in place and ready," Bolan said.

"Blue in place and ready," Conray said.

Another reason green was a stupid color. *Neither* squad was green. And even combined, red and blue should've been purple.

"No further breach pods at space," the L.T. said. "Confirmed. This is it, boys and girls. Shoot straight. Take prisoners if you can."

"Aye, sir!" Bolan said it at the same time Conray did, which irritated her. Unfairly, and she knew that, but the man just *bugged* her today.

"Oh. Right." The L.T.'s voice shifted, like his mouth had gone all flat the way it did whenever he had bad news. "We just got word on the bridge that the ship's cat... Carbine is its ... is *his* name. Cat's loose and about. Try ... try not to kill it ... *hurt* it. Try not to *hurt* it. And..."

The L.T. took that special kind of deep breath Conray remembered all too well from her time in the marines. It was the sigh that only came when a junior officer – or noncom, of course – had to deliver an order from a senior officer that he found, in his professional opinion, idiotic.

Sure enough, when the L.T. spoke again, his tone matched Conray's expectations exactly for delivering that kind of news. Flat, and with a sense that the words were being dragged out of his mouth against the better judgment of his lips.

"And if any of you happen to see this cat in a danger zone, you are to do your level best to protect it from all harm."

The L.T.'s next words weren't intended for them. They were a little distant, like he was covering his mic and didn't think they'd hear him.

"That's gotta be good enough, right? I mean, you don't want them jeopardizing the ship or the cargo for a *cat*."

A pause that was longer than it had any right to be.

Another one of those breaths and a cleared throat. "Yes, sir." Louder, speaking to them again, he said, "If you see said cat, take whatever risks you must. At all costs, allow no harm to come to this cat."

"Say again?" That was Bolan talking, but Conray almost asked the same question.

"You heard me, sergeants. If you see the captain's cat, don't let it get hurt. Understood?"

"But, sir—" Bolan started, but never got to finish.

"I said, *understood*, sergeants?"

"Understood, sir!" Conray said. This time, a fraction of a second before Bolan got those same words out.

"That is all," the L.T. said. "Good hunting."

The lower click of the connection cutting.

"All right, shooters," Conray said to her squad. "I have good news and bad news. Good's that there's just the two breach pods, and we get one of them to ourselves. Bad's that if you see the captain's cat, you're to protect it like it's made of corbonite."

"What does this cat look like, sergeant?" That was from Johannsson. The squad joker. She didn't have to see his face to hear his smile.

"It's got four legs, Johannsson," she said. "You know, like the rats and dogs you see at family reunions. But *un*like your relatives, someone loves this thing. So you see something white and fluffy—"

"Ship's cat incoming, sarge!" That was from Morrison. On the ramp to the deck above.

Naturally, this was when Conray heard the clang of the escape hatch falling clear.

Breach party was incoming.

And so was that damned cat.

7

____

Of all the varieties of two-legs that Carbine had encountered
– and he'd encountered a great many in his time – the carapace two-
legs had to be the strangest.

Such as the ones he approached right now, coming down the
ramp to the lower part of his domain, where he would find Scruffy in
the Humming Place. And, in all likelihood, Home as well.

Some were crouching, as though preparing to pounce on something Carbine couldn't see. But many of these carapace two-legs were
lying on the floor. Belly down.

Now, Carbine could understand lying on the floor. Certainly it
was a fine thing to do, if one was sufficiently tired, and if a particular
patch of floor felt sufficiently comfy at the time.

But surely, the floor here wasn't so comfy that the better part of a
pack of carapace two-legs just *decided* to flop right here.

Certainly, it didn't feel especially comfy under Carbine's paws.
And Carbine was an *excellent* – some might even say *unparalleled*, and
they would be right to say it – judge of comfort.

No, this floor was hard, cold, and too smooth. Like most of the
floor in Carbine's domain. And the air here, if anything, was chillier
than it was in other parts of his domain.

But that wasn't all.

If they were *going* to flop together on this not-particularly-comfy patch of floor, why in Bast's name would they spread out to do it? Why would they not snuggle together, sharing warmth and comfort?

It just made no sense at all. Even for two-legs.

And to do it right underneath more of the flashing noise monsters, that made even *less* sense.

And that *still* wasn't all. They were – every single one of these carapace two-legs – holding sticks.

Now, Carbine had nothing at all against sticks. That *had* to be understood about him. He was, in fact, quite fond of them.

Sticks often danced for his amusement. Sometimes Home made them dance. Sometimes it was Scruffy. Sometimes Svelte. Sometimes a few of the other members of the pride even played with Carbine that way. Making the stick dance while Carbine pounced and batted and bit at it.

Yes, sticks could be great fun.

And some sticks were even *better*. They did *more* than dance on their own.

Some sticks had *dangly toys*.

Oh, but those were the best sticks. The ones with little toys like feathers or fake mice or even just bright shapes that felt good to catch and bite.

Yes, there really was no beating the sticks with dangly toys.

But even though every single one of these carapace two-legs held a stick, not one of these sticks had a dangly toy. Which was just criminal, to Carbine's way of thinking. Which was, of course, the right way to think.

And that wasn't all.

Oh, that was not all indeed.

For, despite the sheer number of sticks being held by these flopping and crouching carapace two-legs, not *one* of those sticks was dancing.

Not for them.

Not even for Carbine.

Why, they held those sticks as though sticks were *boring*. A drudgery they had to endure, rather than a joy they could embrace.

Which just went to show that carapace two-legs really were ignorant. Even among the two-legs, who, as a whole, all too often failed to grasp even the simplest joys of life.

Why, many of them did not even appreciate *sunbeams*.

They had *so much* to learn from cats. If only they'd pay enough attention.

Well, Carbine had no time to teach these...

What was that?

Something was *hissing*.

Wait.

That wasn't a *proper* hiss. There was no inflection to it. No *meaning* to it. That hiss was like...

Was like...

Primal memories surfaced in Carbine's mind, as they did from time to time. Knowledge passed down through the cats of old to the cats of today, as one day Carbine's own knowledge would pass down.

That hiss was closer to a *snake* hiss. Long. Drawn out.

Snakes were dull of wit, but sharp of tooth. In the sandy places, ancient cats did battle with snakes. And some said that those who went to Bast would battle snakes in the afterlife, as well, from time to time.

Well, snakes were most certainly *not welcome* in *Carbine's* domain.

He would have to see about this.

Carbine accelerated his trotting down the ramp.

There was something odd about that snake, wherever it was. First, because it had impressive breath. Not easy, holding a hiss this long. Even for a snake.

But more than that, the smell was odd.

Ancient information told Carbine that snakes smelled dry. With a kind of musk that would suit the taste of their scales, and the spice of their blood.

But this hissing snake, it smelled different. Sour, like cream not worth tasting.

No. Not quite that.

More like...

More like prey meat that had been left in the rain during a thunderstorm, and was just past the sweet phase of decay.

Yes. That was as close as Carbine could come to understanding that smell.

And it didn't smell like the snakes of old.

Well, then Carbine would have the pleasure of being the first cat to kill this *new* kind of snake.

But before he even reached the flopping carapace two-legs, the hissing stopped. And it wasn't followed by a rattle. Nor a slithering sound. Either one of which would have suited the words of the cats of old.

Instead, it was followed by a loud, metallic *clang*. And shuffling, heavy feet. Like the movements of many heavy two-legs.

Oh. Two-legs. Of course. They often found ways to make strange sounds and smells that even their own bodies could not produce.

Perhaps Carbine would not get to face a new kind of snake after all. Pity. After the frustration of being unable to bite the king of the flashing noise monsters, he *longed* to sink his fangs into something that bled.

Wait. One of the flopping carapace two-legs was looking at Carbine. Mewling something to its kin. Now several of them looked his way.

One of them rose to its feet.

Oh, no. Not that again.

Bad enough that *Surly* had dared wrangle Carbine's delicate fur – fur still entirely too disheveled from nap time and rushing about without a bath.

No *way* was Carbine letting a carapace two-legs get hold of him.

Then things got complicated.

There were quick whining sounds, and flashes of light, and smells of heat. And more smells of rain and lightning.

The sticks. These flashes and smells were coming from the sticks held by the carapace two-legs.

What kind of game were they playing?

Oops! No time for that now.

Carbine danced right away from the grasp of a reaching carapace two-legs. Fast as a paw strike he darted left between its legs.

Cut right again past *another* reaching carapace two-legs.

He jumped off the head carapace of yet another.

Into the many-directions spot. Surrounded by carapace two-legs now. But down here, most of them were flopping with their smelly, flashy, whiny sticks.

Some of them were mewling things, too.

It was all so strange that Carbine – yes, even that great unflappable combatant and navigator himself, the amazing Carbine – got turned around for a moment.

Please don't tell anyone. The world would be diminished by the mere idea that Carbine could be less than perfect, even for a moment.

But Carbine turned to dart down *the wrong passage.*

This was a narrow passage. And twisty. And there were more carapace two-legs ahead. But these smelled wrong. And not just the sticks they carried – which were also sadly deficient in dangly toys, by the way.

No, *these* carapace two-legs didn't smell like pride. They'd been eating the wrong food. Sharing the wrong smells and markings.

What was going on here?

Carbine darted back and forth quickly, near the entrance, while all around him came loud yowls from the different groups of carapace two legs. Combined with all the quick whines and flashes and smells, it was very confusing.

Really, *anyone* might've gotten turned around.

But just then, one of the new carapace two legs offered a toy.

It was a strange toy. Larger than most. Maybe as large as Carbine's head (without fur or ears). And it looked hard and smooth, as though it wouldn't feel good to dig claws and teeth into.

But it was shaped like a ball. And sometimes Home would throw such things for Carbine. Smaller ones, of course. And usually made of softer material that felt good to bite, or smelled of sweet catnip.

This ball just smelled like metal and something unpleasant.

But strange as it might have been, it was a toy nonetheless. And hard ball toys sometimes felt good to bat around and chase. Furthermore, *this* toy represented an offering of play from the new two-legs. Refusing the offer would be *most* impolite.

And Carbine was a polite cat, of course.

So he watched as the strange carapace two-legs threw the ball. Quick and bouncing his way.

And Carbine knew *just* what to do when someone threw a ball toy his way.

Faster than a bolt of lightning, Carbine whipped a paw and knocked that toy right back where it came from. So the carapace two-legs who wanted to play could throw it again.

It was a bad toy, really. Too heavy. Batting it hurt Carbine's paw. A pain demanding a few immediate soothing licks.

Someone who smelled like pride snatched up the bathing Carbine in hard, carapace arms.

Dove away from the narrow passage.

Held Carbine up as he – she? Hard to tell under all that carapace – hit the floor.

Something *boomed* so loud it hurt Carbine's ears.

That was the final straw.

Playful newcomers or not, Carbine needed to get out of here.

He wriggled free of the carapace two-legs. Darted swiftly down the ramp and away.

The next level would lead to the Humming Place. And Scruffy. And maybe even Home.

And hopefully no more carapace two-legs.

8

Engineering was usually Merrygold's happy place. But not right now. And not just because of the blaring red light from the action alert.

Right now there were *too many* lights flashing red. Too many screens showing dead. Too many sweet, reassuring hums, vibrations, clicks and whirs gone silent and still.

Too many important systems and subsystems offline.

The main engineering bay was hexagonal, bi-level and sectioned off to provide workstations covering all twenty-four of the *Quick Sail's* primary and secondary systems.

Tertiary and other subsystems were handled in bay two, but right now Merrygold had left only one junior engineer in there, minding the store, while the others were over here, helping her deal with the chaos these pirates had wrought.

In fact, she had eleven of her people down in the tubes right now, digging through the ship's guts. Looking for any and all circuits blown out by that EMP. And working hard enough at it that even at this distance, she could smell their sweat over her own. Not to mention hearing them curse.

And they were just getting started.

Pirates were bad enough. Smart pirates though? There might not be any worse scourge of the space lanes.

And whatever else might be said of the group attacking the *Quick Sail*, they were smart. Merrygold had to give them that much.

They hadn't launched missiles. They hadn't shot lasers or hard beams. They hadn't done any of the things that might do serious, long-term damage to the ship.

Nope.

This group had managed to hit the *Quick Sail* with *targeted* EMP.

It had taken nearly a quarter hour just to confirm that was what happened. Couldn't be helped, though. Neither Merrygold nor anyone under her command had ever *heard* of such a thing. Didn't know the tech *existed* to just pinpoint which systems the pirates wanted to shut down.

But there was no denying its effects.

Knocked out their shields. Knocked out their weapons. Knocked out their *engines*. Knocked out the ship's comms, external and internal. But it *hadn't* taken down their sensors, environmentals, grav, or maintenance systems. All of those readouts were in the normal range.

Most of all, it hadn't taken out their *computers*.

Which meant there had to be *something* in the ship's databanks that they wanted as much as they wanted the cargo. Maybe more.

Oh, God, what was the captain carrying *this* time?

Bitch with Harnan was, it could've been anything from the location of some secret treasure stash to schematics for some new Argalian battleship to the lock codes for Imperial Princess Zeneria's private hangar.

There was just no way to guess what that man was up to.

Well, not for *her* to guess. *Someone* had guessed. And that someone had sent a pretty darned creative pack of pirates.

In fact, Merrygold would've been in awe of their ingenuity. If she hadn't been the one responsible for getting those systems back online ASAFP.

So Merrygold jumped from station to station, trying everything she could think of to work a reboot from the controls and software side while her people were chasing down hardware issues.

After all, there was always a chance that a targeted EMP was weaker than a general one. Might knock the systems out without blowing any – or at least few – circuits and connectors.

Which meant she might be able to get things moving again from the workstation end.

Unfortunately, the only system responding to Merrygold's tricks so far was the one that one took forever to reboot. Comms. Too many rules to process, covering which comm station could do what, on whose authority.

Not to mention that it would also have to then verify the current command passcodes from the main computer banks, which, of course, were still online.

Wait. Passcodes...

There was a duplicate set of command passcodes in the comms system. Not all of them, of course. Only the ones that dealt with communications.

But that might be enough to work with, if the pirates failed to hack the main computers.

People tended to create their passcodes in patterns, after all. And some would even use the same code multiple places.

Having the comms down was good for the pirates during the attack. Kept their prey from calling for help. Isolated the different parts of the ship. Or at least, slowed them to typing and screen reading speed. Which, under duress, was always slower than people wanted it to be.

Certainly too slow to be useful in combat.

But the pirates *might* want the comms to come back online easily. If they were planning to take the ship...

Reminded her of something one of her old instructors used to say at the engineering academy on Cortalis Prime: *Sometimes, my little wrenches, the fubars come in bouquets.*

Good old Instructor Edmundson. Definitely knew her business.

Merrygold shivered from the cold as she checked the comms

status. Only three percent of the way through the boot-up sequence. Great. They were coming up even slower than normal.

Three percent wasn't worth much. But with the main computers still online, she could work with it. That was enough for her to code in a kill switch.

A one-key command to take those comms right back down.

She shivered again as she typed furiously. Freaking cold down here right now.

Local environmentals were kept tuned cold, to take advantage of the heat spillage from the engines. Her own idea, that. Meant that even the least greasy newbie wrench could tell something was wrong with the engines, if the bay got cold.

Merrygold didn't need that little telltale, of course. She could tell by sound when something was off in her engines, even before she checked their readings.

Part of what itched at her right now was the dead silence coming from those engines. And combined with that cold, the silence formed an irritating reminder that *the entire ship* could end up just as dead as those engines, if she and her people didn't get these systems back online at speed.

Most of these systems, anyway.

Targeted EMP.

How the hell could they do that?

More than that, even *with* a targeted EMP, how the hell could they shut down the engines without shutting down the sensors?

That should've been impossible.

In engineering, schematics ruled. That was fact. *Real* schematics, that was. The ones mapped out by clever engineers after the ship was operational. Not the daydreams of the designers that didn't always survive the shipbuilders' reality.

And the laws of routing handed down by the true schematics of *this* ship made clear as vacuum that if connections between the power plant and the engines died, the sensors lost power too. Just like the weapons and shields and comms.

Those systems were all part of the same chain.

But somehow, the EMP had gotten around that. And Merrygold would've *loved* to know how they pulled that off.

Figuring that out could be the key to the whole—

"Mrrr-ow?"

The inquisitive sound was so sudden that Merrygold whipped her head around too fast. Wrenched her neck.

Side effect of getting yanked out of sleep by that goddamn breach alert. Adrenaline might've woken her up and gotten her moving, but not all of her own dependent systems were up to speed yet...

She grimaced more than smiled at the fluffy white cat who stood there in the middle of the bay. Head and tail high as he looked up at her, but fur every bit as disheveled as Merrygold's own uni.

And Merrygold was constantly getting ribbed by the other senior officers about the rumpled, greasy state of her uni. And her hair, for that matter.

Carbine, on the other hand, was usually the portrait of a well-put-together cat.

Well, Merrygold could spare the cat a moment. Her kill switch was ready, and most of her dead boards still showed no signs of life.

"What are you doing here, Carbine?" she said, crouching down and holding out her fingers. "Smart kitties bunker down when an action alert sounds."

Carbine came over and nuzzled her fingers, then started sniffing at them with great interest.

"Oh," Merrygold said, with dawning realization. "This is your first *breach* alert, isn't it? Did that piercing sound hurt your ears? Did that big bad breach alert wake you up and make you go look for the captain? Is that what that sound did?"

Carbine didn't answer of course, but accepted some petting that straightened at least some of his fur.

"Well," Merrygold continued, "I'm afraid I can't spare you time to play right now. And I don't have any treats with me. And Captain Harnan's not here. He's on the bridge."

For some reason that only made sense to the feline brain, Carbine turned and jumped up onto one of the workstations. The shields station.

"Whoa!" Merrygold said, diving forward to grab the kitty before he...

Well, the station was dead. He couldn't really do any damage right now.

Same was true for the weapons system, which he jumped to next. As though taunting Merrygold with what she hadn't fixed.

Wait! Not the comms!

While Merrygold had wasted a precious nanosecond lamenting the state of the ship's weapons and shields, Carbine turned and leaped onto the comms station.

Triggering the kill switch.

Merrygold dove helplessly and too late while yelping a sound somewhere between pain and anger and frustration as the ship's comms shut back down completely. Undoing the little good that Merrygold had been able to—

Wait.

Carbine ran off as Merrygold considered the twice-dead station.

Shields, weapons, comms, the cat had jumped onto. Same order as the schematics dictated, following the engines.

Merrygold had managed to boot a system that shouldn't have had power. Not unless auxiliary power was back up...

A quick glance confirmed it. The auxiliaries were still down too, and they were a chain unto themselves.

But the point was, they were *down*. And so were the engines.

Which meant it shouldn't have been possible to reboot the comms. Not with dead engines. Engine power came first.

And the *computers* were still live...

That was it!

It wasn't some new kind of EMP after all! It was a fake out. The pulse, the flare, the little shiver of the ship. *All* those things could be produced from the software end, by someone who knew what they were doing.

Someone must've snuck onto ship at the last port. Fed in a

program with a remote trigger to *mimic* an EMP strike on certain systems, including mimicking the ship's response to such a hit.

And the pirates had timed the trigger to their fake-EMP light show.

Merrygold laughed breathlessly. Damned clever. And a lot easier to pull off than a targeted EMP.

Of course, that meant someone on the crew had blown a watch rotation and let this happen. And when Merrygold got her hands on them...

But first, she had a job to do.

She stuck two fingers in her mouth and blew the *get your asses in here* whistle that would summon her crew out of the tubes at best speed.

They had an attack program to chase down...

9

The problem in the Humming Place had been clear as water the moment Carbine had entered.

Well, *almost* the moment he entered.

The first thing he noticed was that Home wasn't here. Hadn't been here for quite some time. Which meant that Home hadn't come to consult with Scruffy after all. Which was sad. And it meant that Carbine would have to try to decide which of Home's favorite places he'd be holed up in...

But before Carbine could give the notion much thought, his keen – yet delicate – ears and amazingly quick mind sussed out the problem with the Humming Place.

It wasn't humming.

Oh, there were a *couple* of hums, and maybe a click or two. But really, it was so quiet that – if Carbine didn't know better – he would've thought it should've been called the Quiet Place.

And no sooner did Carbine notice this – which was probably a good deal sooner than most would have, in his place – than he immediately recognized *why* silence ruled there.

It was the fault of the flashing noise monsters. Obviously. Three of them perched high in the Humming Place. And the Humming Place had very high walls indeed.

What was just as obvious was that almost *all* the flashing lights *normally* found in the Humming Place were gone.

Therefore, the flashing noise monsters had eaten them. Which meant that quick action was called for.

At first, Carbine had assumed that Scruffy understood this. She seemed to be noticing the missing flashing lights and hums. And surely even a two-legs could make the connection to the flashing noise monsters.

But then, she turned and cooed to Carbine, and petted him. Which was welcome, of course. After the day Carbine had had, a little reassurance that Scruffy still loved him felt good.

But that was not the time for reassurance. Not with flashing noise monsters eating all her lights and hums. She needed to take *quick action*.

Then Carbine understood. Scruffy, despite being fairly clever, for a two-legs, had not yet made the obvious connection between the flashing noise monsters and the loss of her hums and flashing lights.

She hadn't been trying to solve the problem. She'd been lamenting their loss.

Carbine, of course, would've immediately pounced on those flashing noise monsters and given them *what for*. If he'd been able to.

But even Carbine, even mighty Carbine – who was a noted leaper even among the most agile of arboreal cats – could not jump high enough to teach those flashing noise monsters a proper lesson.

The walls in the Humming Place were simply too tall. And its shelves and projections simply provided no properly placed imitation tree limbs to facilitate access.

And so, alas, Carbine could not solve this issue *for* Scruffy.

But he *could* bring her attention to the problem.

With that in mind, he leapt up onto a shelf where the hums and flashing lights should've been strong and bold.

Scruffy only yelped and tried to catch him. As though Carbine could possibly *fall*.

Unheard of.

So Carbine reinforced his point. He leapt from dead zone to dead zone. Forcing Scruffy to look at the lost lights and hums.

Then, according to his plan, he would meow loud defiance up at the flashing noise monsters. Try to *force* Scruffy to make the connection between her lost lights and hums and those awful, perching things.

Unfortunately, Scruffy was too fixated on the idea of harm coming to Carbine's person should he accidentally fall.

Patently ridiculous. But still, a sweet thought on Scruffy's part. That she could be so worried about him, even when he wasn't the one in danger. Even when she was losing her precious lights and hums.

But by the third dead shelf, the sound Scruffy made changed. Got sharper. Louder. And she looked up.

She was looking the *wrong way*. There were no flashing noise monsters where she was looking.

But still. She had the right look, and made the right sounds.

She understood *something* of what Carbine was trying to tell her. She must've.

And being a two-legs, Scruffy had height resources to draw on that weren't available to Carbine. She would now be able to deal with her own flashing noise monsters. And maybe help spread the word about them.

Which would have to be good enough. Because fond of Scruffy as Carbine was, he could not stay here and help her battle her flashing noise monsters.

No. Scruffy really *was* fairly clever for a two-legs. And if Scruffy had needed *Carbine* to tell her about the threat posed by the flashing noise monsters, well, then, it had to be admitted that Home might not understand the danger either.

Home, he was even cleverer than Scruffy. Why, at times he seemed to be almost as clever as a cat. A slow cat, surely, but still. Impressive for a two-legs.

But if something were *distracting* Home. Holding his attention on, perhaps, the *effects* of the flashing noise monster invasion, he might not have made the connections necessary to realize the *source* of his problems.

Even Home might not understand the danger.

So Scruffy would have to battle her flashing noise monsters without Carbine's aid.

It was no longer just that Carbine needed Home.

Home needed Carbine.

So Carbine had to find him. As soon as possible.

But where? What could so be distracting Home that he might not realize the danger? For now Carbine felt certain that Home must not've understood the threat. Otherwise, by now, he would have either dealt with them, or come to get his Carbine, for assistance.

Oh, no.

Home couldn't be looking for *Carbine* could he?

Carbine spared a moment to wash his face while he considered that question.

It was possible. Certainly. Which meant that Carbine needed to get back to the den. And quick. Home might be there looking for him. Lamenting the absence of his beloved Carbine.

It was the sort of thing Home would do. Which meant that, at the very least, the possibility had to be eliminated as quickly as Carbine could manage.

He'd have to take a different route back, though. Last thing Carbine wanted to deal with was more grabby carapace two-legs, with their big booming noises and whiny, smelly sticks.

Fortunately, Carbine knew this ship like he knew his own tail.

10

———

Easy flight, Harnan had said. *Grain run*, Harnan had said. *No trouble at all*, Harnan had said.

When, oh when, was Perry going to learn?

Whenever *Harnan* says a flight's going to be a grain run, something will go horribly wrong.

Guaranteed. One of the basic truths of life.

Like that each human heart only has so many beats in it. And no matter how many ways people come up with to extend human life, if they don't find some way to fortify the heart so it can handle more beats, no one's going to live past maybe a hundred and twenty.

Equally as basic a truth was that if Harnan was sure he'd gotten them an easy commission, it would be anything but.

At least he'd had the sense to double the ship security for the voyage.

Though admittedly, that was something Perry would have dearly loved to know *in advance*. So he could've taken the hint and stocked up on more of his own supplies.

The Andromeda run.

Perry should've remembered the Andromeda run.

Harnan had said *that one* would be a grain run too. Instead, they got caught smack dab in the middle of a star-system-wide civil war.

Perry'd had drinks with Merrygold two shifts before liftoff, for that run. And Merrygold, she'd had a bad feeling about it. Trusting her bad feeling, they'd both stocked up a little extra. And they'd needed it.

The lesson there was clear.

Harnan talked more to Merrygold than to anyone else on the ship. He'd said something that had clued Merrygold in, in ways no one else could've caught. In some way she didn't understand herself, but intuitively knew meant danger.

Therefore, it could happen again.

Which meant that Perry would simply *have* to make sure he had drinks with Merrygold before leaving planet *every time* they were ready to go on a new run.

Alas, that wouldn't help him now.

He was already short on beds and autodocs. And if those pirates were too well-armed...

Well, no use thinking that way. If they took the ship, they took the ship. All Perry could do was save as many lives as possible.

Fortunately, so far, most of the casualties reaching Perry's med bay were pirates, not crew. And while Perry didn't want *them* dying on him either, at least they'd been *asking* for trouble in attacking the ship.

Right now, the badly injured filled all six of his med bay beds, and ten others were...

Well, ten others didn't *need* beds. Four because their injuries were too light. Never make it past triage to Perry's own attention. His team was too good for that.

Even now, he could hear their soothing, professional voices, talking in low tones to their patients. Could smell the antiseptics dealing with their relatively minor cuts and abrasions.

As for the other six not in beds, well, they'd been dead on arrival.

Six beds would *not* be enough, though. Not if the fighting kept up.

Even here in the med bay, just bridgeward of amidships, Perry had felt vibrations from the explosion that had killed those pirates and wounded more of them back by the cargo bay. And though he couldn't hear the whines, he would have sworn he could smell the sour ozone of hard beam rifles...

No good worrying about that. He had patients to deal with.

The four pirates in his beds were kept sedated, while the autodocs worked to keep them alive.

Too much for the autodocs in at least two cases. Perry was almost positive, but had just enough doubt that he had to try to get them to the point where he could perform surgery that might save them.

Their chances were slim, though. He could smell the perforation of bowels in both cases, and he was not at all sure security had gotten them here in time for the autodocs to help.

For that matter, he wasn't at all sure that the security team had *tried* to get them here in anything like a reasonable time frame.

Reminded Perry of the warning he'd gotten from both his father and grandfather, back when he'd first decided to become a medic in the service, instead of going into private practice, as they had.

Pay someone to kill, and they slowly stop valuing life.

Father and Grandfather both had said it. And while Perry didn't think it was true in *every* case, experience had told him it was true more often than he liked to think.

At least, when those lives didn't belong to friends and allies...

"How're we doing over here?" Perry said, pushing a smile past his mood as he approached the two conscious patients in his autodocs. Both members of his own crew.

Morrison's autodoc was covering her lower half. She'd taken a bad burn to her left thigh, and a little concussion damage and shrapnel to both her calves. Apparently sustained – according to her, at least – diving to save the captain's cat from a grenade.

If so, that meant she valued the life of a cat more than some of her companions valued the very human lives of their enemies.

What did that say about soldiers?

Or perhaps that was too general. Perhaps the question ought to have been, what did that say about her?

"Better now, sir," she answered, smiling. It was a goofy kind of smile. A mixture of relief, disbelief, and pleasure.

The smile of someone who'd been in intense pain before the painkillers kicked in.

"Am I going to be able to keep my legs?" she asked. Still smiling, which meant maybe she was getting more painkillers than she needed...

Nope. A quick check of the autodoc's monitors confirmed that she was getting exactly the right amount, given her height, weight, gender, genetic background, and injuries. Taking into account, of course, the nerve-deadeners that allowed the autodoc to work on her tissue.

Perry made sure not to give her a glib answer. Too quick, and, even in her drugged state, she'd assume he was lying. Too slow, and she'd worry more than she should, even if it were good news.

So he made a show of checking her readings.

"Looks good, spacer," Perry said. "You should still have both legs the next time you need to save a cat. Though I strongly suggest doing all your therapy before doing any more cat diving."

"If it's the captain's cat in trouble," she said, smiling even wider, "I'd do it again right now. Saved our whole squad, he did."

Perry chuckled. "Maybe your painkillers *are* set a little too high."

"They're not, doc." That was from Andres, in the next bed.

His voice was a little weak, but he sounded surprisingly lucid. He'd taken a pair of nasty hard beam shots to the chest. Said good things about his armor that he was still alive. But even flexiplate had its weak spots.

"Oh?" Perry said, stepping over and checking Andres' readouts on the autodoc. He was shorter than Morrison, so the bed's autodoc covered him from neck to knees, even though it was only working on his upper chest. "Sounds like you're angling for more painkillers yourself."

Readings looked good. He'd be on his back the rest of the trip, but he'd live. Might not even need Perry to suit up for surgery.

"I wouldn't say no," Andres said, grinning. "But I mean about the cat. Damndest thing I ever saw. The grenade was bouncing our way—"

"It was going to go off *right* in the intersection," Morrison said urgently.

"Would've killed most of us," Andres said, nodding. All humor gone from his face. "But that cat *smacked* it with his paw."

"Sent it *right back down* the twisty emergency passage," Morrison said, her face a mixture now of humor and sheer wonder.

"*Carbine* did that," Perry said, voice full of disbelief. He'd never known that cat to move any faster than it needed to, and only then for food or attention.

"Is that his name?" Andres asked.

"If so," Morrison said, "Carbine's a—Hey! There here is!"

She raised a shaky hand to point, and sure enough, there was that little white fuzzy troublemaker, trotting right past the wide, med bay doors as though he had something important to do.

"Grab him!" Andres said, sounding entirely *too* awake and lucid, given what was pumping through his veins.

He'd even started trying to sit up! Despite the autodoc holding him down!

"He's fine," Perry said, trying to soothe the man back supine.

"No!" Morrison said, sitting up herself. "He's heading toward the other breach! Johannsson! Get him!"

"Now *really*," Perry said, but one of the men receiving light treatment actually nodded at Morrison and jumped to his feet, flexiplate dangling off his scarred — *and* newly cut up — torso.

"I'll get him," he said, grabbing his rifle and slamming his helmet onto his head.

Perry's assistant looked up at him, antiseptics and bandages still in hand. Every bit as surprised as Perry.

Surely all this fuss was unnecessary anyway. Surely a cat was smart enough not to go near a skirmish.

But that man, Johannsson apparently, took off down the passage double-time. Armor still hanging open from the treatment he'd been receiving.

"Attention!" Perry snapped. "Next patient of *mine* who risks further harm and trouble going after a *cat* is going on *report*!"

He gave them all the Doctor Glare that settled them back down.

But to Perry's amazement, they grumbled about it.

11

HOME HAD NOT BEEN IN THEIR DEN. AND THE DEN DID NOT SMELL AS though he'd been there since Carbine left.

Further, that smelly old thing that Carbine had – quite unintentionally and through no fault of his own – knocked down from the fun shelves earlier remained on the floor where it had fallen.

Home would definitely not have left it there. He never did, when something happened to fall from the fun shelves. For one reason or another.

And to Carbine's way of thinking, if Home wasn't back in their den looking for Carbine, and he wasn't defending the food, and he wasn't fighting the flashing noise monsters, and he wasn't consulting with Scruffy, that meant poor Home didn't understand the danger he was in. The threat level represented by these awful, flashing things, whose littermates seemed to have scattered themselves all throughout Carbine's domain.

Indeed, Carbine had yet to find anyplace where they didn't perch and flash. Silently, after the beating Carbine had given their king, but still menacing all the same.

Even now, they perched high on the walls near Carbine and flashed down at him, threateningly.

If Home didn't understand the threat represented by the flashing noise monsters, then he was in *danger*. And he needed his Carbine to come *save* him.

Unfortunately, this meant Carbine first had to *find* the great silly two-legs.

But Carbine had an idea about that.

Home had a chair that let him look out the big window. And he could spend *hours* in that chair. Watching little lights moving past and talking with other two-legs.

Carbine didn't understand that. The lights weren't very interesting. They didn't swoop and perch like birds. And they didn't look as though they'd be very tasty, or even feel good under one's teeth.

And yet, Home seemed to find them endlessly entertaining. And so did many of the other two-legs of the pride. Because it was rare that Home was staring out his window without at least a half-dozen other two-legs around. For company. And perhaps to enjoy the lights.

All very strange, but if Home liked it, that was fine with Carbine.

The point was, if Home didn't understand that he was in danger, he might be watching his lights moving past his window. Which meant Carbine had to check that place next.

Unfortunately, getting to Home's window place from the den meant passing by the Dread Place.

Carbine *hated* the Dread Place.

Strangely, one of the pride's two-legs, Stoic, seemed to like the Dread Place. Which made no sense at all.

Stoic himself was all right. Not very friendly, really, but he always treated Carbine with respect. Even if he steadfastly refused to pet him or play with him or even speak gently to him.

He was respectful, though. And he never acted as though Carbine were guilty of some *great imagined wrong*. The way Surly did.

So Stoic himself was decent enough. Mostly. But he was a little suspect. Not because of anything he, himself, had done. But because of the place he'd chosen as his favorite.

The Dread Place.

The Dread Place was *all wrong*.

It smelled of pain and fear and blood and death. The very air there tasted of it, even when the place was empty of two-legs.

Fear and blood and death were only good smells when they came from prey animals, offering up their sad little lives to sustain more important people. Like Carbine. Or Home.

Come to think of it, pain could be a good smell. When it came from a prey animal.

Sometimes it was fun to play with prey animals, before killing them. And at times like those, the smell and sound of their pain and fear could be a purr-worthy joy.

But that was different.

The Dread Place, it had *nothing* at all to do with prey animals or joy. No, the fear and blood and pain and death smells coming from that place all too often came from those who otherwise smelled like *pride*.

And when those smells came from pride...

No. Stoic and his Dread Place were not to be visited willingly. They were to be avoided.

Carbine wanted nothing to do with that place. And honestly, he couldn't understand why Stoic did. It said bad things about him.

And frankly, if Carbine didn't know what wonderful two-legs Home and Scruffy and Svelte could be, he would've worried about what it said about *them* that they allowed Stoic and his Dread Place to remain in Carbine's domain.

But not one of them seemed interested in chasing Stoic away.

Why would that be?

Perhaps Stoic was not the problem?

Perhaps the *place* was bad, and Stoic was its *guardian*? Keeping its awfulness from spreading throughout Carbine's domain?

That made some sense.

And if that was the case, then it explained Stoic and his behaviors. Had to take a lot out of him, being the Guardian of the Dread Place.

Carbine would have to make allowances, in Stoic's case. Maybe even pay him some attention. Perhaps come sit on his lap and nuzzle him, the next time he visited the den or the food place, or wherever Stoic, Home and Carbine might all gather at the same time.

Yes, Stoic was probably starved for affection. Being the Guardian of the Dread Place.

Well, next time, Carbine would ensure that Stoic knew he understood.

But not now.

No. Even reassuring Stoic would not be worth stopping in at the Dread Place. Especially when Carbine *had* to find Home.

So Carbine shuddered only a little – purely in sympathy for Stoic's plight and not out of any fear of his own, of course – as he neared the Dread Place.

And he sped his pace, so that he would have to smell the awful smells – which were *even worse* than normal that day – as little as possible as he made his way toward Home's window place.

But as Carbine passed the Dread Place, he heard the cries of two-legs. They mewled and yowled to one another. And Carbine would've thought they were cries of pain, but he heard the boots and rustling of a two-legs coming to its feet.

A *carapace* two-legs. Face strangely visible. Long stick dangling for a moment, before being hung over a shoulder.

Which just proved that some two-legs didn't understand sticks *at all.*

Worst of all, part of its carapace hung open. And foul, biting smells came from within. Not the smell of blood – well, there was *some* of that, but it was weaker. Older. No, this foul, biting smell only ever came from the Dread Place.

And it was sharp. Bit at Carbine's nostrils and tongue, promising suffering.

And that carapace two-legs was *coming after Carbine.*

Oh, no. No more of that. Carbine had had more than his fill of big, stupid carapace two-legs trying to grab him, thank you very much.

Too-smooth floor or no too-smooth floor, Carbine bolted away.

That carapace two-legs was *not* catching this cat!

12

There were times in Bolan's life when the whine of hard beam rifles was the sound of a sweet symphony. When the hot, dry smell of their shots made his mouth water like the call to mess after a long engagement.

Right now was one of those times.

He had those ship-thieving bastards right where he wanted them. Nowhere near ramps up or down. Pinned down into two corridors, with his team split to cut off half their escape routes. Conray and the remains of her team covered the other two.

Had those bastards in a crossfire. And there wasn't much they could do about it.

They'd already tried one of their grenades.

Mackenzie had charged it. Bolan had thought she was going to dive on it. Take it for the team. But she didn't. Just changed the grip on her rifle and yelled something about carbines.

Made no sense. Their rifles weren't carbines.

Anyway, that woman must've played baseball or cricket or something back on Denas Three, because she batted that grenade right back where it came from with perfect form.

Hit it too well, actually. Sent it down the hall and into an open door, where it went off in some cabin.

Bolan had no idea what cabin that was. But his people had survived the grenade, and that was what mattered. He'd already lost too many to rad burns in this fight. *Despite* the new armor.

These ship thieves were fighting like the damned.

But at least they hadn't tried another grenade.

In fact, it was that grenade – well, all right, the grenade *and* the arrival of Conray with the remains of her team – that had turned the tide. Given the sec teams a clear edge.

Now it was just a matter of time.

"Mac, give me a count," Bolan said, pulling back his rifle to hold tight to the cover of his corner while three hard beam shots whined past.

"At least six breachers still fighting," she said, from one knee on the opposite corner from him. "Ten down that I've seen."

"Conray," he said into his helmet mic. "We need to press in."

"No cover in those halls. It's a death zone. Better to hold position. Pick 'em off."

"We need to wrap this up."

"I'm already down eight from two fights," she said, and Conray sounded agitated with him for some reason. "If we push, you're doing the pushing."

"I'm down four myself," Bolan snapped back. "And if we don't push from all sides, it won't work."

"Of course it will," she said. "Pressure is pressure."

"We need to wrap this up," Bolan said again, more urgently.

"Hurrying a battle's a good way to make extra corpses," Conray said.

Sounded like she was quoting someone. Always reading books on military theory. Complete waste of time. Anyone who knew anything about warfare knew that *experience* was the only teacher worth a damn.

Bolan shook his head. "Are you going to help me or not?"

Conray's sigh just pissed him off. Like she was smarter than he was. The big sister putting up with her little brother's nonsense.

"Let's be smart about it then," she said. "Which direction's the breach pod?"

"Doesn't matter. I'm not letting them escape."

"Don't be an idiot. If they don't think they have a way out, they'll fight to the death."

"I hate ceding conquered ground," Bolan said through clenched teeth.

"Ceding... Are you saying the breach pod's behind you?"

Bolan leaned around the corner and returned fire before pulling back.

"Now who's the slow one?" he said.

"Did you search the pod?" she asked.

"Been a little busy." He nodded at Mackenzie who took her turn firing.

And damn it, from her smile she hit one. One *Bolan* might've hit, if Conroy wasn't yapping in his ear.

"But you have guards on it?" she pressed. Apparently having no problem pressing *him*.

"Haven't had the manpower to spare."

"What the—"

"What?"

"Captain's cat inbound."

"Oh, you've got to be *kidding* me," Bolan said, but Conray cut transmission.

She wasn't seriously endangering this op for a freaking *cat*.

Couldn't have been.

Bolan opened contact again.

"Hate to say this, Conray, but we're in the middle of something *important*."

She didn't answer him.

Suddenly the firefight went crazy down the corridor. From little barrages of three or six shots came a frenzy of nonstop shooting.

This was it! Conray was charging! Trying to steal the glory of *his* idea!

"We're going!" Bolan said through his mic to his team. "Advance on both fronts! Shoot to kill!"

With a roar, Bolan charged into the corridor, rifle up and firing. Mackenzie and the rest of his team right on his heels. Spread out, for the clearest possible lines of fire.

Their boots clanged on the deck like the charge of a thousand angry soldiers across a field of steel.

Screams from up ahead. Some of them pain, but many were screams of ... fear?

What the hell was happening up there?

Breachers tried cutting across the passage. Fleeing something. Rifles held for running speed, not for shooting. Not even looking toward Bolan and his charging team.

Bolan didn't need to give the order. He and his soldiers opened fire.

Two thirds of those breachers never made it across the passage.

More were coming. Bolan called the halt. Had his people take firing positions.

It was like shooting at the range.

And his people were really good at the range.

No more breachers successfully crossed the passage. The intersection now littered with their dead and wounded.

"Mac?"

"Yeah, sarge?"

"Your count was low."

"Could only count what I saw," she said with a shrug. "More must've been trying to push Conray's teams."

"Whatever," Bolan said. "Everybody up. Darius, Orin, check the intersection."

Darius and Orin moved ahead, rifles ready.

Hey! Orin had stopped shaking. Maybe he'd last after all.

They'd almost reached the corner when a fluffy white missile ran past.

Bolan almost shot it.

Orin tried to.

Missed, thankfully. Because it was that damned cat again.

This time, it was being chased by…

Well, Bolan didn't know who that was, but he was wearing the right armor. Or most of it, considering his helmet visor was open and his chest piece dangled uselessly behind him. And the man looked positively terrified by the possibility of something happening to that cat.

In fact, he stopped in the intersection. Turned wide, furious eyes on Orin.

Started stomping toward the rookie like he was intent on murder.

"Stand down, soldier," Bolan ordered, pushing forward.

"But this idiot—"

"I said *stand down*."

"Yes, sergeant."

"Name."

"Johannsson, sergeant."

"You're with Conray, right?"

"Yes he is," Conray said, stepping into the intersection. With two quick gestures, she had members of her team checking the downed ship thieves.

Conray turned to Johannsson. "You're supposed to be in med bay."

"But, sergeant," he said, turning to her, "the cat—"

"Save it," Conray said, raising one hand. "I understand. But if you're going to do that cat any good, you can't stop and discipline this idiot."

Orin turned fuchsia.

"Hey!" Bolan snapped, angry flaring through him. "You don't get to talk about my people that way."

Conray didn't even look at him.

"Get moving," she said to Johannsson, then turned a glare on Orin that made him fall back a step.

Johannsson took off after the cat.

Conray held her glare on Orin, but spoke, at least, to Bolan.

"What would you do if this idiot fired on a crew member? No. Not just a crew member. A sec squad member?"

"Look," Bolan said. "I get that the captain loves his cat—"

"You get *nothing*, Bolan," Conray said, finally turning to face him. "That cat saved my squad back at the other breach. And we owe *this* fight to him too."

"Ridiculous."

"But, sarge," Mackenzie said softly to him. "Word on the comms said—"

"I know what it said." Bolan shook his head, unable to believe that *anyone* on his team would buy that load of bilge. "We won this fight because *my* team —"

But Conray talked over him.

"I don't know what the dying pirates said about that cat over their own comms." She pointed at the dead and wounded. "But *this* lot got one look at him and turned tail."

"Oh, right."

"Maybe they thought he was *carrying* a grenade." She sounded pensive now.

"Sarge?" one of her people said from the bodies of the ship thieves. "Most of these are dead, but four are still alive. We need to get them to med bay."

She nodded. Turned back to Bolan. "Discipline your man. He just tried to shoot the hero of the day."

Orin had paled now, and looked unsteady on his feet.

"I'll handle my own team, thank you," Bolan said.

Conray looked him up and down with distaste.

"Fine then," she said. "But see about that breach pod you left behind. Might be trapped."

She turned away then as though dismissing him.

Bolan almost hauled off and hit her. But that would've set the wrong example for his people.

And it didn't help that Darius and Mackenzie were looking at

Orin like he was guilty of everything Conray'd said. And they weren't the only ones giving him that look.

Fine then. Let Conray have her moment.

When this was all over, though, he would have to teach her a lesson in manners, when addressing one's *peers*.

13

Nothing about this day was going right.

There was chaos everywhere in Carbine's domain.

Ultimately, of course, that was the fault of the invading flashing noise monsters. But now Carbine was beginning to wonder how much culpability he really ought to assign to the carapace two-legs.

They were running wild today. All over his domain, carrying those sticks that they steadfastly refused to play with.

Crouching on floors. Lying on floors. Making strange, whining sounds and weird, summertime sandy place smells. And some of them making burned or bloody or even death smells. And often mewling and yowling at each other.

And not all of them were even pride.

One of them – who did smell like pride – was chasing Carbine. Had been since the Dread Place. Possibly even wanted to force Carbine *into* the Dread Place.

Which could. Not. Happen.

Carbine would've lost him long ago, of course. Except for these unfortunate, too-smooth floors.

They were fine for straightaways. Well ... not *fine*, but not much of a problem. Meant more skittering than Carbine liked, but that couldn't be helped.

No. The real problem was cornering.

Carbine had the most wonderful claws any cat was ever blessed with. And he kept them in pristine condition, with a great deal of scratching and cleaning.

On just about any surface Carbine had ever experienced, he could use those claws to corner so tightly, even other cats couldn't keep up with him.

On a *proper* surface, that chasing carapace two-legs – whose face and torso were still strangely visible – would never have had a chance.

Carbine would've lost him by the first corner, and the last thing the big, slow, clumsy two-legs would've seen was the fluffy white tip of Carbine's tail, disappearing.

But alas, Carbine's domain did not have proper surfaces. Only these too-smooth floors that felt too hard under his claws.

No chance of gaining purchase. Of handling cuts and turns with the kind of grace and agility that Carbine truly possessed.

Instead, turns were a skittering, sliding mess. Even leading to a roll once in a while, about which *we shall not speak.*

No. Because the floor worked against Carbine, even that slow, clumsy – yet persistent – carapace two-legs could *almost* keep up with him. Pushed Carbine to maintain speeds that, well, made cornering tricky.

Tricky enough that Carbine had missed the turn he'd most wanted to take. The turn that would've led through two narrower halls – halls filled with hums and *normal* flashing lights – to a final stretch leading to Home's favorite window room.

And with that carapace two-legs lumbering after him – intentions unknown but surely foul – Carbine couldn't risk trying to turn about on this too-smooth floor.

He might've been caught.

Nope. Nope, nope, nope. Not. Happening.

So Carbine had been forced to stick to wider halls and fewer turns.

And this ... this led to the single weirdest thing to happen to him all day.

Carbine found himself approaching a pack of crouching carapace two-legs. They were all looking the other direction, so he didn't think they'd be a problem. Carapace two-legs were hardly the most observant creatures in the world.

But he hadn't counted on the ridiculous racket made by the great lumbering carapace two-legs chasing him.

They definitely heard that.

Many of them turned. Some even raised their sticks for some reason.

What were these things? Comfort sticks?

...no. No, that still didn't make sense. Sticks provided comfort through play.

But then they started mewling and yowling to one another. And Carbine heard them make that sound that meant his name.

Well, it was good that they recognized the master of their domain, he supposed. But the way a couple of them moved then, they might've wanted to grab him.

And *obviously* that could not happen.

So Carbine cut loose.

Up until this point, Carbine had been holding back from his maximum speed. Just in case he needed some kind of emergency maneuvering that would not be possible for *anyone* at the kinds of speeds that Carbine could run.

And with a veritable forest of carapace two-legs coming for him, pure speed was his only chance.

So he poured it on. Pumping with all four paws at top speed. Belly safely low. Tail streaming out behind him. Head at just the right height to minimize wind resistance.

Not that there was ever a proper wind in Carbine's domain.

Still, instincts were what they were.

And at top speed, Carbine bolted past them.

Many of them immediately followed him.

Up ahead, more carapace two-legs. Strangers. They didn't smell like pride. But Carbine was *not* about to risk that they'd try to grab him. So he kept up his blurring speed.

And they started running too. Not *after* Carbine, though. Away from him.

The sweet smell of their fear reached them.

That was a prey smell. And they ran with abandon. Like prey...

Maybe this was an invitation to play the chase-me game. Maybe these non-pride carapace two-legs were actually a new form of prey animal.

Either way, the smell of their fear and the speed of their desperation lent fresh power to his legs and focus to his mind.

Then things got even weirder.

Those hot, summery sandy-place smells got stronger again.

And the carapace prey two-legs started falling. Some smelled of pain. More smelled of death.

Was this Carbine's doing?

Maybe.

No time to consider it. He focused on the living prey and pushed harder.

More of them fell.

And more.

Until finally, all the prey carapace two-legs were down.

But more approached from down a side hall. These smelled like pride though. And they didn't smell of fear at all.

But they might try to grab Carbine, so he never slowed.

He pushed on right past them.

Something sizzled the floor near him, but by the time Carbine realized that had happened, he was thirty steps past and running.

He left the carapace two-legs behind him. Even the lumberer, who'd been chasing him since the Dread Place.

But he no longer mattered anyway. Because now Carbine saw the section of wall that would open for him, letting him enter Home's window room, straight ahead of him.

There were more dead carapace two-legs on the floor next to the wall there.

Carbine jumped over them. Trusting that the wall would open for him, as it always did.

It did, thank Bast.

Which meant that at least *one* thing had gone right for Carbine that day.

14

Captain Edrik Harnan paced at his command station.

The bridge of the *Quick Sail* was too small for proper pacing. Even here, at the widest spot, he could get only five steps each direction before he had to turn around.

He ought to just take his seat. He knew that. But he couldn't sit still. He wanted to be out there himself. Battling pirates, as he had so many times before.

Why oh why had he let his security chief, "Lieutenant" Mills talk him into disarming the bridge?

Yes, it was the command center. And yes, it was important to coordinate from here.

But that wasn't exactly easy with the comms down, now was it?

They had the computer message system, but apart from Mills' headgear mic, that was it.

Mills could talk to her team leaders, but no one else.

Harnan shot another glare at her. She was tall, strong and smart, but this time she'd outsmarted herself. And she'd brought him along for the ride.

Olson, over at navigation, looked jumpy. Poor kid. Good navigator, but not used to action situations. Couldn't stop his knees from bouncing. And there wasn't much he could do right now beyond plot courses they couldn't follow.

"Olson," Harnan said. "Be ready. Merrygold'll get those engines back online any time now, and we need to be ready to go."

"Yes, sir," Olson said, turning back to the nav comp.

"Reed," Harnan said, addressing his pilot next. Might as well go station to station, and make something productive out of his pacing.

Reed looked up at him. Feral grin already gracing her features. As eager to grab a rifle and get out there as he felt himself. But that wasn't where he needed her.

"Second those engines get back online," he said, "go full on port thrusters. Let's burn those pirates for boarding us."

"Yes, sir," she said, her grin now the one he remembered from that fracas on Qintal Two. She'd saved his bacon that time. Shot that syndicate killer that had been sneaking up on him.

Oh, the celebration they'd enjoyed later that night, just the two of them, that memory was worth an entirely different kind of smile.

But Harnan turned to the last major station on the bridge, apart from his own.

"Yandu," he said, addressing his weapons officer.

"I know, sir," Yandu said, with a fighting grin of his own. "Second we have enough safe distance, hit them with everything we've got."

"Good man," Harnan said, clapping him on the shoulder.

"Cat update," Mills said, turning from her station. She had her poker face up, which meant it was good news. She was a terrible poker player.

"Go," Harnan said eagerly.

"Carbine..." Into her mic she said, "Say again."

Harnan stepped closer.

Mills shook her head.

"Apparently, Carbine somehow panicked the breach team into bolting. Made them easy prey. And right now he's headed—"

The bridge door opened.

"—this way."

Carbine ran in and straight to Harnan. Wasting no time, he jumped right up into Harnan's arms.

Harnan, smiling, held his fluffy cat against his chest, scritching his ears and cooing, "You got into all kinds of trouble today, didn't you?"

Carbine looked up past Harnan's shoulder and let out his troubled meow.

Something had really bothered the little guy. But that would have to wait a moment.

Turning back to Mills, and in his normal voice again, Harnan said, "Status?"

"All breachers dead or captured, sir. Breach pods clear. Teams are detaching them and re-sealing the hull right now."

"Excellent. Kill the alert."

"Yes, sir," Mills said.

The alert lights stopped flashing. Which seemed to settle Carbine, for some reason.

Harnan continued petting him all the same.

"Engines back online!" Reed called, triumph in her voice.

"Merrygold, you're a certified genius!" Harnan said.

Reed shot him a grin. "Better grab a seat, sir."

Harnan, smiling, took his command chair while Carbine settled onto his lap, purring.

Sure enough, his own control board showed systems coming back online quickly. Engines back at half, and restoring quickly. Shields already at three-quarters. Weapons ... missiles ready, but hard beams only at thirty percent and climbing.

No comms yet. Probably still booting.

He fired off a quick message through the computer system, advising all crew to strap down for initial velocity.

Not as good as announcing over the comms, but some would see it, at least.

"Yandu," he said. "Give me shields, heavy port side."

"Shields, aye." That was Yandu. All business, now that he had a live board again.

"Engines ready?"

"Ready," Reed said, sounding eager to do some damage.

"Go!"

Reed hit the port side thrusters, shoving the *Quick Sail* hard away from the pirate cruiser, burning it in the process.

Carbine's claws dug into Harnan's thighs. Not that Harnan would let the little guy fall. Held him with one hand, petted with the other.

"Missiles!" he said. "Second we're clear."

"Three..." Yandu counted, deadpan. "Two. One. Missiles away."

Harnan watched as the pirates – apparently only just realizing that the *Quick Sail* was back in the fight – tried to get their shields up.

Too late.

Four missiles of, well, in *some* places it was legal for civilian vessels to carry missiles of that potency, slammed point blank into the pirate cruiser.

"Four hits," Yandu said. "Major hull breaches in all four places. Engineering damaged. Environmentals, weapons, shields, all damaged heavily."

"Ready hard beam follow-up."

"Targets selected," Yandu said. "When shall I fire."

"When you can pack a punch."

"At this range ... waiting for sixty-percent power."

"Agreed," Harnan said. "Olson, got our course ready?"

"Yes, sir." Olson stared white-faced at Harnan. Poor kid did *not* handle combat well.

Harnan gave him a patient look, but the kid didn't get it.

"Care to feed it to my station then?" Reed asked with a warning smile that looked sweet, if you didn't know her.

"Right! Sorry." Olson turned back to his station and did his job.

"Reed," Harnan said, "get us out of here, in case they can call in friends."

"Firing," Yandu said. "Pirate engines down. Weapons too. And shields. Continue firing?"

"No," Harnan said. "I'd say they're out of the fight."

Carbine mewled an objection when Harnan stopped petting him

long enough to type at his keyboard. But he needed Derek down in comms to contact the boys in red as soon as comms were back online.

With any luck, though, by the time Space Enforcement and Compliance arrived, the *Quick Sail* would be long gone.

After all, while his *missiles* might be legal in some places, they weren't legal *here*.

Not to mention his cargo. Morphozine ultra was a controlled medicine under imperial law, because they didn't want anyone else to have their precious wonder drug.

But people were dying out in the border worlds. Sure, some of them rebels – not that Harnan was all that worried about politics – but many of them just because the empire didn't seem to care.

Well, Princess Zeneria cared. Cared enough to get Harnan a full load of morphozine ultra to haul out there. And Harnan could no more let the boys in red take it away from him than he could let pirates.

For that matter, he didn't need either of them knowing she'd also given him the new codes for her private hangar...

15

No sooner did the wall open and admit Carbine into the room with the big window than he saw and smelled Home.

Already moving at speed, Carbine simply ran to Home and jumped into his arms.

Home caught him just right, of course, and immediately snuggled him in close to his chest. Petting Carbine and cooing to him. Filling Carbine with the kind of happiness that only Home could provide.

The purr almost overwhelmed Carbine. Carried him away into bliss.

But Carbine needed to *focus*.

Home didn't understand the *danger* he was in.

So Carbine looked up at the flashing noise monsters, perched high on the walls, and let loose a warning yowl. The best yowl he had left, after this long, demanding day.

And Home, of course, reacted just right. Knew immediately that something had upset Carbine. And that Carbine was looking right at it.

Home knew to take *quick action*.

Now, Carbine wasn't sure exactly what that quick action was. To

Carbine, it looked like little more than mewling something to Long, one of the female two-legs on the bridge.

But the two-legs, they did things in a strange, roundabout way sometimes. And this seemed to be one of those times.

Well, whatever it was that Home did, sure enough, it worked.

The flashing noise monsters stilled and died.

They flashed no more. They shrieked-buzzed-honked no more. Their corpses merely hung there in their perches. Dead and useless. Not even good food.

Carbine would leave them right where they perched, though. To serve as a warning to others of what happened to any who dared to threaten Carbine's domain.

Yes, they would provide a *fine* example.

And now, with their threat ended, peace would once more spread through Carbine's domain. Perhaps even the carapace two-legs would settle down...

Just then, the wall opened and that carapace two-legs with the strangely visible face and torso ran into the room.

He stood, panting, paws braced on his knees. His stick falling to the floor, hanging down from a string in the exact opposite of the way sticks were supposed to work.

But he saw Carbine in Home's arms, and settled down.

Home mewled something to that carapace two-legs, who answered in kind. The sound Home made then was a good one. A peaceful, pleased sound.

That...

That must've meant that this carapace two-legs had been trying to *help* Carbine. Perhaps that Home had sent him to *find* Carbine, and bring him.

Well, why hadn't the great lumbering oaf merely communicated that in the first place?

Two-legs could be especially slow sometimes. And carapace two-legs seemed to be the worst of the lot in that regard.

But that didn't matter.

What mattered was that together, Carbine and Home had won the day again.

Home seemed to understand now that the danger was past, and sat. Holding Carbine on his lap for some proper attention.

Well, with minor distractions so Home could mewl at other two-legs, or play with that box that perched in front of his chair.

But those things didn't matter.

Carbine and Home were together. The threat of the flashing noise monsters had ended.

And once more, all was right in Carbine's world.

SIGN UP FOR STEFON'S NEWSLETTER

Stefon loves to keep in touch with his readers, and loves to keep you reading. The best way for him to do both is for you to sign up for his newsletter.

Sign up at http://www.stefonmears.com/join

If you sign up for Stefon's newsletter, you get...

- Monthly updates about his publishing and travel schedules
- His latest news, in brief, and answers to reader questions
- A free short story for signing up
- List-only offers and occasional specials
- Plus a free short story every month!

ABOUT THE AUTHOR

Stefon Mears has seen his cats battle a variety of flashing noise monsters over the years. Stefon has more than thirty novels to his credit, and he never stops writing. He earned his M.F.A. in Creative Writing from N.I.L.A., and his B.A. in Religious Studies (double emphasis in Ritual and Mythology) from U.C. Berkeley. He's a life-long gamer and fantasy fan. Stefon lives in Portland, Oregon, with his wife and three cats.

Look for Stefon online:
www.stefonmears.com
himself@stefonmears.com

9 781948 490504